The Tennis Twins

By Shaun Gayle   Illustrated by Patrick Owsley

VICTOR BOOKS

A DIVISION OF SCRIPTURE PRESS PUBLICATIONS INC.
USA   CANADA   ENGLAND

Dear Parents,

The influence of time is tremendous. What is heard and seen every day will have some type of effect on our kids. Whether our children spend time with us, or with others, we need to make sure it's in accordance with certain moral standards.

What was inexcusable ten years ago is commonplace today, making the potential of tomorrow less than it should be. This can change by and through our children, but it's our responsibility to help them. We cannot know what our children may experience in our absence, but we can find comfort in using the opportunity to teach them beyond the mathematics and history lessons of a school curriculum. This can only happen through a commitment of time and effort.

We have to talk and listen to our kids: find out if they know what racism is; explain the importance of sacrifice and compassion; teach them the meaning of perseverance and faith; give them the moral foundation that seems to be disappearing in our society. We have to provide for them what we may not have had ourselves—realizing that anything we leave to chance is a chance we cannot afford to keep taking.

These books have specific themes with an emphasis on Christian values. Though the meaning of each book could be easily taken for granted or even overlooked, we should not minimize the importance of teaching our children lasting values that must overshadow the inevitable influences of time spent away from us.

I hope you and your children will read these books with each other and enjoy an investment of time well spent.

For my mother, Delores,
my grandmother, Catherine,
and my brother, Jimmy.

—S.G.

To my family, Kristine, Lindsay,
and Kirby for their never-ending
patience and support, and to Jack
Davis for the inspiration!
Congratulations to the newlyweds,
Stephen and Tracy!

—P.O.

Somewhere, in the big city during warm summer nights,
city kids gathered to play tennis under the lights.

The sounds of the city were so distinct and clear
the subway and the trains always seemed easy to hear.

The games the kids played were fun in their own way—
like stickball and basketball which they played each day.

But tennis was a game they could play all the time—
in the morning or afternoon even without sunshine.

The kids loved to play those games in the street,
but tennis at night helped them avoid the summer heat.

Tennis was really fun, and everyone loved to win.
The kids liked the competition and no one ever gave in.

Even though they weren't the best players in the world,
the best of the group was this one little boy and little girl.

They were in many matches and had lots of wins.
They played great together because they were twins.

One night, as usual, while they were having a good time,
two new boys boasted, "We're the best you'll ever find."

Everyone watched the twins and the boys play,
but the twins were too good in almost every way.

The twins had soundly beaten them three games to one,
and while they were doing it, they seemed to have fun.

The kids told the twins how tough they were to beat,
but it was the little boy who claimed he caused their defeat.

"We play well together as you can probably see,
but the reason we beat everyone is because of me.

"Everyone knows a boy is better than any girl.
Everyone knows that–everyone in the whole wide world!"

But the little girl said, "No way. That's just not true.
You're not better than me. In fact, I'm better than you.

"Just because you're a boy doesn't mean you're better than me.
Girls can do what boys do and even be what boys want to be."

"I can be a fire fighter, an astronaut, or even a truck driver too.
Girls can be what they want to be and do whatever they want to do."

The little boy said, "I don't know what you can be,
but I do know in tennis you can't beat me."

"You're my sister and you're good—yes, that is true.
If you think you're better, let's play and I'll show you."

As they began playing, all the kids watched the court—
enjoying their effort and the way they played the sport.

The little girl was fearless as she played that game,
proving to her brother their talent was not the same.

The kids began to laugh. Even the little girl started to grin,
realizing the little boy was losing, and she was going to win.

One boy said, "Hey! You can't possibly lose to a girl!
That's a terrible thing—the worst thing in the world."

But she looked at her brother and noticed his face,
his look of embarrassment, his look of disgrace.

She wanted to show her brother something—without the shame,
knowing his feelings were more important than any tennis game.

So she stopped the match before it was done,
as they both understood she'd have easily won.

She said to her brother, "I just wanted you to see
just by being a boy doesn't mean you're better than me."

The game was over and they'd both played really well
proving talent is what matters—not being female or male.

Shaun Gayle is a veteran Chicago Bears football player with a "heart for kids." A graduate of Ohio State University with a degree in education, Shaun Gayle has been with the Chicago Bears since 1982 and is an integral part of the Bears' defensive force. He was captain of the victorious 1985 Super Bowl XX team and in 1984 was the recipient of the Brian Piccolo Award.

Patrick Owsley holds a B.A. in illustration from Columbia College in Chicago. He has done cartoon illustrations for magazines, advertising, greeting cards, coloring books, and comic books, and currently works on staff as an "in-house" letterer for Malibu Comics Entertainment. He lives in Southern California with his wife Kristine and two daughters.

Discover all the *Shaun Gayle's Sports Tales* at your local bookstore. Book/cassette packages also available.

The Little Quarterback, Home Run Pete, Jonathan McBoo, Jill and the Hill, The Golden Shoe Goalie, The Tennis Twins

Cover design: Scott Rattray
© 1995 by Victor Books/SP Publications, Inc.
Text © 1995 by Shaun Gayle.
All rights reserved. Printed in the USA.
1 2 3 4 5 6 7 8 9 10 Printing/Year 98 97 96 95

VICTOR BOOKS
A division of SP Publications, Inc. Wheaton, Illinois 60187